THE SPIDERWICK CHRONICLES

TROLL TROUBLE
SPECIAL EDITION OF THE SEEING STONE

VOLUME TWO
with EXCLUSIVE LOST CHAPTER

Tony DiTerlizzi *and* Holly Black

Simon and Schuster Books for Young Readers
New York   London   Toronto   Sydney

SIMON AND SCHUSTER UK LTD
Africa House, 64-78 Kingsway, London WC2B 6AH
A CBS Company

Originally published in the USA by Simon & Schuster
Books for Young Readers, an imprint of
Simon & Schuster Children's Division, New York.

This edition published exclusively for
Nestlé breakfast cereals 2007

The text type for this book is set in Cochin.
The display types are set in Nevins Hand and Rackham.
The illustrations are rendered in pen and ink.

A CIP catalogue record for this book is available from the
British Library

ISBN-10: 1-84738-158-8
ISBN-13: 978-1-84738-158-3

Printed and bound in Great Britain by
Clays Ltd, St Ives plc

Table of Contents

Welcome to our daring tale,
but there's a little twist:
This book is not the very start.
That's right. There's stuff you missed!

THE GRACE KIDS

So let us take you back in time,
back to our starting place,
where you can meet our heroes three—
Mallory, Simon, and Jared Grace.

They'd left the city far behind
and moved out to the sticks,
to a musty, dusty old estate
with the name of SPIDERWICK.

And no sooner had they settled in
than mysteries arose.
A secret room! A long-lost book!
A houseguest filled with woes!

And, oh, the woe this creature caused!
And, oh, the grief and shame,
for every prank this rascal pulled,
poor Jared got the blame.

THE
BOGGART

But that lost book was filled with clues.
When found, it set things right.
And in that secret room a brownie
stepped into the light.

He cautioned our young heroes three
of troubles deep and drastic
if they kept the book, Spiderwick's guide
to worlds close and fantastic.

THIMBLETACK

But young Jared heeded not,
saw nothing to be feared,
until before his very eyes
his brother disappeared.

He asked the brownie Thimbletack
for aid finding a stone
that saw into the hidden world
in which his twin had gone.

GOBLIN

Through mischief Jared got the rock
and found his goblin foe,
then fought them off with Mallory
and thus our status quo.

Since Simon needs to be rescued,
and Thimbletack appeased,
Jared and Mallory set out
beneath the autumn leaves.

SPRITE

What will they find along the way?
Dear reader, turn within
to find what mysteries await
just around the bend.

The air was different.

Chapter One

IN WHICH Jared and Mallory Find Many Things, but Not What They're Looking For

Stepping into the woods, Jared felt a slight chill. The air was different, full of the smell of green things and fresh dirt, but the light was murky. He and Mallory stepped through tangles of jewelweed and past thin trees heaped with vines. Somewhere above them a bird started calling, making a harsh sound like an alarm. Beneath their footsteps, the ground was slick with moss. Twigs snapped as they passed and Jared heard the distant sound of water.

There was a streak of brown, and a small owl settled on a low branch. Its head cocked toward them as it bit into the small, limp mouse in its claw.

Mallory pushed through a knot of bushes, and Jared followed. Tiny burrs caught on his clothes and in his hair. They sidled around the crumbling trunk of a fallen tree swarming with black ants.

There was something different about his vision with the stone in place. Everything was brighter and more clear. But there was something else, too. Things moved in the grass, in the trees, things he couldn't quite see but was aware of for the first time. Faces made of bark and rock and moss that he only saw for an instant. It was as though the whole of the forest was alive.

"There." Mallory fingered a broken branch

and pointed to where clumps of ferns had been trampled. "That's the way they went."

They followed the trail of smashed weeds and snapped branches until they came to a stream. By then the woods had grown more shadowed, and the twilight sounds had increased. A cloud of gnats settled on them for a moment, then blew out toward the water.

"What do we do now?" Mallory asked. "Can you see anything?"

Jared squinted through the eyepiece and shook his head. "Let's just follow the stream. The trail has to pick up again."

They walked on through the forest.

"Mallory," Jared whispered, pointing at a huge oak tree. Tiny green and brown creatures were perched on a branch. Their wings resembled leaves, but their faces seemed almost human. Instead of hair, grass and flower buds grew from their tiny heads.

"What are you looking at?" Mallory raised her rapier and took two steps backward.

Jared shook his head slightly. "Sprites . . . I think."

"Why do you have that stupid expression on your face?"

"They're just . . ." He couldn't quite explain. He extended his hand, palm up, and stared in amazement as one of the creatures alighted on his finger. Soft feet tickled his skin as the tiny faerie blinked up at him with black eyes.

"Jared," Mallory said impatiently.

At the sound of her voice, the sprite jumped into the air. Jared watched as it spiraled upward into the leaves above.

The patches of sunlight filtering through the trees became tinged with orange. Up ahead,

the stream widened where it ran under the remains of a stone bridge.

Jared could feel his skin prickle as they got closer to the rubble, but there was no sign of goblins. The stream was very wide, almost

One alighted on his finger.

twenty feet across, and there was a darkness in the middle that seemed to speak of deep water.

Jared heard a distant sound like metal grating against metal.

Mallory stopped, looked across the water, and raised her head. "Did you hear that?"

"Could it be Simon?" Jared asked. He hoped it wasn't. It didn't sound human at all.

"I don't know," Mallory said, "but whatever it was, it's got something to do with those goblins. Come on!" With that, Mallory bounded in the direction of the noise.

"Don't go in there, Mallory," Jared said. "It's too deep."

"Don't be a baby," she said, and waded into the stream. She made two long strides and then dropped as though she had stepped off the edge of a cliff. Dark green water closed over her head.

Jared lunged forward. Dropping his rapier onto the bank, he plunged his hand into icy cold water. His sister bobbed to the surface, sputtering. She grabbed for his arm.

He had pulled her halfway onto the bank when something began to surface behind her. At first it seemed like a hill rising from the water, stony and covered in moss. Then a head emerged, the deep green of rotten river grass, with small black eyes, a nose that was gnarled like a branch, and a mouth full of cracked teeth. A hand reached toward them. Its fingers were as long as roots, and its nails were black with murk. Jared breathed in the stench of the bottom of the pool, putrid leaves, and old, old mud.

He screamed. His mind went completely blank. He couldn't move.

Mallory pulled herself the rest of the way onto the bank and looked over her shoulder.

Something began to surface.

TROLL

"What is it? What do you see?"

At her voice, Jared snapped into moving and stumbled wood-enly away from the stream, tugging her along with him. "Troll," he gasped.

The creature lunged after them. Long fingers dragged through the grass just short of where they were.

Then the creature howled and Jared looked back, but he couldn't see what had happened. It felt toward them again but jerked away when one long finger fell into a beam of light. The monster bellowed.

"The sun," Jared said. "It got burned by the sun."

"There's not much sun left," Mallory replied. "Let's go."

"Waaait," the monster whispered. Its voice was soft.

Yellow eyes regarded them steadily. "Cooome baaack. I haaave something for youuu." The troll extended a closed hand as though something might indeed be clutched in its palm.

"Jared, come on." Mallory's voice was almost pleading. "I can't see what you're talking to."

"Have you seen my brother?" Jared asked.

"Perhaaaps. I heard something a tiiime ago, but it was bright, too bright to look."

"That was him! It must have been. Where did they go?"

The head swung toward the remnants of the

bridge and then looked back at Jared. "Cooome closer and I will tell you."

Jared took a step back. "No way."

"Aaat leassst cooome geeet youuur sss-word." The troll gestured to the rapier beside itself. The sword was lying on the bank, where Jared had dropped it. He looked over at his sister. Her hands were empty too. She must have left her sword at the bottom of the pool.

Mallory took a half-step forward. "That's the only weapon we have."

"Cooome and taaake it. I will clooose my eyeees if it will maake you feeel saaafer." One huge hand covered its eyes.

Mallory looked at the sword in the mud. Her eyes focused on it in a way that made Jared very nervous. She was thinking about trying for it.

"You can't even see the thing," Jared hissed. "Let's go."

"But the sword . . ."

Jared untied the eyepiece and held it out to her. Her face went pale at the sight of the massive creature, peeking through a gap in its fingers, imprisoned only by the fading patches of sunlight.

"Come on," she said shakily.

"Noooo," called the troll. "Cooome baaack. I'll eeeven tuuurn aroooound. I'll coooount to ten. It'll beee a faaair chaaance. Come baaaack."

Jared and Mallory ran on through the woods until they found a patch of sunlight to stop in.

25

Both leaned against the thick trunk of an oak and tried to catch their breath. Mallory was shivering. Jared didn't know if it was because she was soaked or because of the troll. He unzipped his sweatshirt, took it off, and handed it to her.

"We're lost," Mallory said between gulps of air. "And we're unarmed."

"At least we know they couldn't have crossed the stream," said Jared, struggling to tie the eyepiece back on his head. "The troll would have gotten them for sure."

"But the sound was on the other side." Mallory kicked a tree, chipping off bark.

Jared's nose caught the scent of something burning. It was faint, but he thought it smelled like scorched hair.

"Do you smell that?" Jared asked.

"That way," Mallory said.

They crashed through the brush, heedless of the scratches twigs and thorns made along their arms. Jared's thoughts were all of his brother and fire.

"Look at this." Mallory stopped abruptly. She reached into the grass and picked up a single brown shoe.

"It's Simon's."

"I know," Mallory said. She turned it over, but Jared couldn't see any clues, except that it was muddy.

"You don't think he's . . ." Jared couldn't bring himself to say it.

"No, I don't!" Mallory shoved the shoe in the front pocket of her sweatshirt.

He nodded slowly, allowing himself to be convinced.

A little farther, and the trees began to thin. They stepped out onto a highway. Black

A single brown shoe

asphalt stretched off into the distant horizon. Behind it all, the sun was setting in a blaze of purple and orange.

And on the shoulder of the road, in the distance, a group of goblins huddled around a fire.

Sinister wind chimes

Chapter Two

IN WHICH the Fate of
the Missing Cat Is Discovered

Jared and Mallory approached the goblin camp cautiously, dodging from trunk to trunk. Broken bits of glass and gnawed bones littered the ground. High in the trees they could see cages woven from thornbushes, plastic bags, and other refuse. Squashed soda cans hung from the branches, clattering together like sinister wind chimes.

Ten goblins sat around a fire. The blackened body of something that looked like a rat turned on a stick. Every now and then one of

"Skin it raw, skin the fat."

the goblins would lean over to lick the charred meat, and the goblin turning the spit would bark loudly. Then they would all start barking.

Several of the goblins started to sing. Jared shuddered at the words.

> *Fidirol, Fidirat!*
> *Catch a frog, catch a rat*
> *Skin it raw, skin the fat*
> *On the spit, turn like that*
> *Fidirol, Fidirat!*

Cars whizzed by, oblivious. Perhaps even their mother was driving past now, Jared thought.

"How many?" Mallory whispered, hefting a heavy branch.

"Ten," Jared answered. "I don't see Simon. He must be in one of those cages."

"Are you sure?" Mallory squinted in the direction of the goblins. "Give me that thing."

"Not now," said Jared.

They moved slowly through the trees looking for a cage large enough to contain Simon. Ahead of them, something cried out, shrill and loud. They crept forward to the edge of the forest.

An animal was lying alongside the road, beyond the goblin camp. It was the size of a car, but curled up, with a hawk's head and the body of a lion. Its flank was streaked with red.

"What do you see?"

"A griffin," said Jared. "It's hurt."

"What's a griffin?"

"It's kind of a bird, kind of a—never mind, just stay away from it."

Mallory sighed, moving deeper into the woods.

"There," she said. "What about those?"

Jared looked up. Several of the high cages were larger, and he thought he could make out a human shape in one of them. Simon!

"I can climb up," Jared said.

Mallory nodded. "Be fast."

Jared wedged his foot in a hollow of the bark, hefting himself up to the first split in the branches. Then, pulling himself higher, he started crawling along the bough that held the little cages. If he stood up on that limb, he would be looking into the cages that were hung higher.

As he edged along, Jared could not help looking down. In the cages below, he could see squirrels, cats, and birds. Some were clawing and biting at the bars, while others were unmoving. They were all lined with leaves that looked suspiciously like poison ivy.

"Hey, dribble-puss, over here."

The voice surprised Jared so much he almost lost his grip on the branch. It had come from one of the large cages.

"Who's there?" Jared whispered.

"Hogsqueal. Now how about opening that door?"

Jared saw the frog face of another goblin, but this one had green cat's eyes. It was wearing clothes, and its teeth weren't glass or metal, but what looked like *baby* teeth.

"I don't think so," said Jared. "You can rot in there. I'm not letting you out."

"Don't be a cat-whipper, beetlehead. If I holler, those guys are going to make you into dessert."

"I bet you yell all the time," Jared said. "I bet they don't believe anything you say."

"HEY! LOOK—"

Jared grabbed the edge of the cage and pulled it forward. Hogsqueal went quiet. Below, the goblins slapped one other and snatched pieces of raw meat, apparently unaware of the racket in the tree.

"Okay, okay," Jared said.

"Good. Let me out!" the goblin demanded.

"I have to find my brother. Tell me where he is, and then I'll let you out."

"No way, candy butt. You must think I'm as dumb as a hatful of worms. You let me out or I scream again."

HOGSQUEAL

"Jared!" Simon's voice called from one of the cages farther down the branch. "I'm over here."

"I'm coming," Jared called back, turning toward the sound.

"You open this door or I scream," the goblin threatened.

Jared took a deep breath. "You won't scream. If you scream, they'll catch me and then no one's going to let you out. I'm getting my brother out first, but I'll be back for you."

Jared edged farther down the branch. He was relieved that the goblin stayed silent.

Simon was stuffed in a cage much too small for him. His legs were drawn up against his chest, and the toes of one foot stuck through the bars. His bare skin was scraped from the thorns that lined the cage.

"You okay?" Jared asked, taking his pocketknife out and sawing at the knotted

"You okay?"

vines wrapped around Simon's prison.

"I'm fine." Simon's voice quavered just a little.

Jared wanted to ask if Simon had found Tibbs, his lost cat, but he was afraid of the answer. "I'm sorry," he said finally. "I should have helped look for the cat."

"That's okay," said Simon, squeezing out through the part of the door Jared managed to open. "But I have to tell you that—"

"Turtle-head! Boy! Enough mouth! Let me out!" the goblin shouted.

"Come on," said Jared. "I said I'd help him."

Simon followed his twin back along the branch to Hogsqueal's cage.

"What's in there?"

"A goblin, I think."

"A goblin!" Simon exclaimed. "Are you crazy?"

"I can spit in your eye," Hogsqueal offered.

"Gross," said Simon. "No, thanks."

"It will give you the Sight, jinglebrains. Here," Hogsqueal said, taking a handkerchief from one of his pockets and spitting in it. "Rub this on your eyes."

Jared hesitated. Could he trust a goblin? But then, Hogsqueal would be stuck in the cage forever if he did anything bad. Simon would never let the goblin out.

He took off the eyepiece and wiped the dirty cloth over his eyes. It made them sting.

"Ugh. That's the most disgusting thing ever," said Simon.

Jared blinked and looked over at the goblins sitting around their fire. He could see them without the stone. "Simon, it works!"

Simon looked at the cloth skeptically but rubbed his own eyes with goblin spit.

"We had a deal, right? Let me out," Hogsqueal demanded.

"Tell me what you're in there for, first," said Jared. Giving them the handkerchief was nice, but it could still be a trick.

"You're not very chicken-beaked for a nib-head," the goblin grumbled. "I'm in here for letting out one of the cats. See, I like cats, and not just 'cause they're tasty, which they are, no mistake. But they got these eyes that are an awful lot like mine, and this one was real little, not much meat there. And she had this sweet little mewl." The goblin looked lost in his memory, then abruptly looked back at Jared. "So enough about that. Let me out."

"And what about your teeth?" Jared had not found the goblin's story very reassuring.

"What is this? An interrogation?" Hogsqueal groused.

"I'm letting you out already." Jared came closer and started to cut the complicated knots on the cage. "But I want to know about your teeth."

"Well, kids got this quaint idea of leaving teeth under their pillows, see?"

"You steal kids' teeth?"

"Come on, Dumbellina, tell me you don't believe in the tooth fairy!"

Jared fumbled for a few more moments, saying nothing. He had the last knot almost sawed through when the griffin started screeching.

Four of the goblins circled it with pointed sticks. The animal couldn't seem to raise itself very far off the ground, but it could snap at the goblins if they got too close. Then the creature's hawk beak connected. The wounded goblin squealed while a second drove his stick into the griffin's back. The remaining goblins cheered.

"What are they doing?" Jared whispered.

"What does it look like?" Hogsqueal replied. "They're waiting for it to die."

"They're killing him!" Simon yelled. His eyes were wide, staring down at the gruesome spectacle. Jared realized that his brother was seeing all this for the first time. Suddenly Simon grabbed a handful of leaves and sticks from the tree they were standing on and hurled them at the goblins below.

"Simon, stop it!" Jared said.

"Leave him alone, you jerks!" Simon shouted. "LEAVE HIM ALONE!"

All of the goblins looked up at that moment, their eyes reflecting a ghostly pale white in the dark.

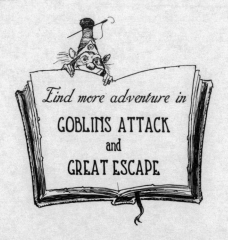

Find more adventure in
GOBLINS ATTACK
and
GREAT ESCAPE

This episode has found its end,
but please don't close the book—
this chapter's new for those of you
who dare to take a look!

Pulled a feather out of its tail

Lost Chapter
TROLL TROUBLE

IN WHICH the Troll's Bridge Is Broken

The troll squatted in fetid water, as if waiting for the sun to slip lower in the sky. Its eyes were black as stones, never even blinking. Thimbletack spotted him as Arthur Spiderwick began packing up his easel and watercolor paints for the day. Thimbletack knew he should say something, point the creature out, but he was worried that Arthur might want to get closer and sketch the troll, or that he might get out some mirrors and try to reflect sunlight at it—which had a very small chance of killing it and a much greater chance of making it angry.

Arthur hated all trolls, but that was understandable, since one had attacked his brother. Arthur had seen the whole thing, but no one had believed him. The newspapers said it was a bear. Since then, Arthur had made it his life's work to collect all the information he could about faeries, in the hopes of informing people and preventing more deaths. People can be very stupid about faeries.

Arthur could be very stupid about faeries too. The best thing to do when near a troll at twilight was to move away before dusk turned to full night. Thimbletack twitched with annoyance and looked nervously back through the woods. He never should have let Arthur persuade him to stray this far from the house.

"What is it?" Arthur asked him.

"The sun is low," Thimbletack said. "Time we go."

"You're as nervous as a rat in . . ." Arthur was forever starting sentences and then forgetting to finish them because of something more interesting occurring to him. He stripped off the contraption he wore over his head. He called the thing a monocle. It held the single seeing stone that allowed Arthur to see faeries.

Thimbletack darted ahead, beckoning to Arthur, making sure he didn't use his own glamour, so that Arthur could see him.

"Yes, yes," Arthur said. He moved slowly, obviously enjoying his leisurely stroll. He stopped to stare at the knot of a tree, inspecting it for signs of faerie habitation. Earlier that day they'd stumbled on a nest of sprites and Arthur had managed to paint several in great detail. He was probably pleased with the day's accomplishment and looking forward to a pleasant dinner with his family.

Looking back, Thimbletack saw the troll creep out of the water, keeping to the shadows. Oh, this was bad. Very bad indeed. But if Arthur kept going, then he'd make it to the house before the sun was all the way down. The troll didn't dare attack before then.

Darting around Arthur, the brownie saw the Spiderwick estate, the windows lit with oil lamps, and Arthur's daughter, Lucinda, catching fireflies on the lawn. The insects darted through the air like sprites. Spinning around, her white dress stained green from the grass, Lucinda seemed utterly distracted by delight. When she saw her father, she waved and ran toward him.

Behind Thimbletack, the troll made a rumbling sound. Trolls weren't bright, but they were fast and shrewd.

"Miss Lucinda," Thimbletack called. "It's cold enough I can see your breath. Go inside, or if you're not careful, you'll catch your death."

"It's a perfectly nice night," Arthur said mildly.

Thimbletack glanced toward the barn, only a few human-size paces to their right, where Arthur kept a few chickens, a rooster, and a rather elderly horse. Maybe if the troll could be persuaded to head in that direction . . .

He looked back. The troll's black eyes stared directly at the little girl as she paused to trap another bug in her hands. She was wandering closer to the troll, the fireflies distracting her from greeting her father.

Thimbletack scolded himself. He should have just told Arthur before. Now the troll was close enough that it might be able to catch her even if Thimbletack yelled a warning.

"Miss Lucinda, go and see," he called instead, "Arthur might have some candy."

Abruptly she veered back toward her father and away from the creature. Thimbletack breathed a sigh of relief.

Lucinda and Arthur began walking across the yard toward the house. Thimbletack wanted to shout. He wanted to tell them to speed up, to run, but he was terrified that they would freeze or look around, or that Arthur would pull out his seeing stone. *Just keep going,* he urged them in his thoughts. But still they dawdled and the shadows lengthened and the troll crept closer.

He needed to think of a way to scare the troll off, but how? His magic might be able to scare off a few goblins, but he had no chance against a troll. After all, what trolls were afraid of was morning, and how was he likely to threaten that with the sun nearly disappeared from the sky.

Then he had a thought. Trolls weren't very bright, were they?

Thimbletack ran to the barn, veering around tall clumps of wild onion as quickly as his little legs would carry him. Then he scrambled under the rough, weather-beaten edge of the door and jumped through the straw and stray cracked corn, startling the chickens to clucking.

Looking around, he spotted the rooster, perched high above the hen's nests, its eyes closed and its tail feathers drooping with sleep. Thimbletack grabbed a post and started to shimmy up it. The splintered wood cut the pads of his hands and caught threads on his overalls.

He thought about the troll gaining ground and climbed faster.

Finally the brownie made it onto the landing. Creeping across the loft floor, Thimbletack snuck closer to the rooster. He was halfway to it when it opened its beady orange-and-black eyes.

He ran right up to the rooster and pulled a feather out of its tail. The rooster crowed and turned to peck at the brownie. Its beak came down savagely only inches from where Thimbletack stood. But the crowing hung in the air, the universal sign that dawn was coming, and soon daylight would pin the troll to whatever shadows it could find.

Hopping to the window, Thimbletack looked out. The troll, who'd lumbered halfway across the lawn, was stopped and squinting in the direction of the setting sun. Then it started

shuffling back toward the water and darkness.

Thimbletack watched as Arthur and
Lucinda entered the house. He could see the
smoke spiraling out of the chimney and imag-
ined them washing their hands and sitting
down to Constance's rosemary roasted
chicken.

Casting a dark look behind him, he wished
for just a moment that Constance was making
rosemary roasted rooster instead. The bird
stared, as if daring him to come within beak
range.

Gingerly, Thimbletack began the long climb
to the floor of the barn, ignoring all the
squawking and flapping of feathers.

The next sunny day, Thimbletack confessed
what had happened. After Arthur finished
yelling, he picked up a sledgehammer and

headed out toward the bridge, muttering some-thing about teaching that troll a lesson.

Thimbletack didn't try to tell him that the troll would just seek shade elsewhere or that it would be made more angry than afraid by Arthur's actions. He was sorry that he hadn't warned Arthur about the troll, but now he remembered why he hadn't.

People could be very stupid about faeries.

Hey, beetlebrains!
Do you want to learn more
about the noddy creatures
in these books?
Then turn the page. . . .

Hogsqueal is a "Common Hob"

HOBGOBLINS

FAMILY: *AMICIDIABOLIDAE*

SPECIES: *Diabolus praestigiator*

PREFERRED HABITAT: Rocky outcroppings, caves, or even ditches along the sides of the roads.

DESCRIPTION: Similar to goblins in appearance, *hobgoblins*, or *hobs* as they are sometimes called, are a less malicious and more mischievous type of faerie.

Friendly and sometimes even helpful, hobgoblins still have a penchant for pranks that can range from annoying to infuriating. They are most fond of stealing trinkets and food, but they also enjoy tripping people and otherwise causing amusing havoc.

Like goblins, hobgoblins are scavengers, but unlike goblins they are solitary in nature and are never spotted in large numbers. It is unclear if they are a wholly different species from goblins or merely the same species with a remarkably different disposition.

The mischievous Puck from William Shakespeare's *Midsummer Night's Dream* identified himself as a hobgoblin. Many times, children and pets are blamed for this creature's pranks and practical jokes.

Griffin fighting a dragon

GRIFFINS

FAMILY: *MIXTIDAE*

SPECIES: *Gryphon americanus*

PREFERRED HABITAT: They like to make homes in high places, preferably in the desert.

DESCRIPTION: The regal *griffin* (also spelled *gryphon*) is thought to be the offspring of an eagle (king of the air) and a lion (king of all beasts). Its plumage ranges from cream to deep brown, yet some species have feathers with a deep, dark bluish sheen.

While many griffins migrated to Europe from the Middle East in the thirteenth century, most remain desert-dwelling. They roost in high places and are only likely to be spotted when they fly in search of food. Their bones are more commonly discovered, although they are often mistaken for the bones of dinosaurs.

The adult griffin is about the size of a lion but far stronger. Despite their formidable natural advantages, griffins are very rare. Unlike less fantastical hybrids like mules, however, they can reproduce. Their eggs are said to be made of agate.